D0888682

TOM
and
JERRY
THE ASTRO-NOTS

by

William Johnston

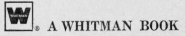 A WHITMAN BOOK

Western Publishing Company, Inc.

Racine, Wisconsin

CONTENTS

CHAPTER   PAGE

1. Jerry's Dream   9

2. Reluctant Volunteer 33

3. Tom Wins Again 57

4. The Isolation Test 81

5. Astronaut Acrobatics 105

6. Whirligig Woes 129

7. Outsmarted 153

8. The Collectors 177

9. No-Fun Fun House 201

10. Last Laugh 225

Jerry Is Restless

CHAPTER 1

JERRY'S DREAM

It was a lazy, restless sort of morning. Jerry was lolling around the house, wandering from room to room, nervously twitching his tail.

The trouble was that he couldn't find any mischief to get into. He had tried, but each time he had failed.

The very first thing that morning, Jerry had attempted to build himself a sandy beach. The idea was to nibble a hole in the corner of the sugar sack, and then, when the sugar ran out, to pretend that it was sand.

But when he started to nibble, he got a grain of sugar in a cavity in one of his teeth. That gave him a toothache and put an end to his plan to build a beach.

Next, he decided to do some water-skiing. He would first fill the

A Toothache

bathtub, he thought. Then, with a couple of Popsicle sticks tied to his hind feet, he would go skiing down the sloping end of the tub. He pictured himself whizzing across the surface of the water.

But it wasn't to be. When he went to the kitchen to get the Popsicle sticks from the kitchen drawer, he found Tom, the cat, sitting in front of the cabinet. Tom looked at him very suspiciously, as if wondering what Jerry was up to. So Jerry had had to give up the idea

Tom Eyes Him Suspiciously

of going water-skiing.

In fact, it looked like the day was going to be a total flop. For right now, Tom was skulking along behind Jerry, following him everywhere he went. Tom was just waiting for Jerry to begin enjoying himself, so that he could pounce on him and put an end to it.

Jerry had just about decided that, as long as he wasn't going to be able to have any fun, he might as well take a morning nap. But at that moment he happened to be

Waiting to Pounce on Jerry

crossing the open newspaper that
someone had left on the floor near
the big easy chair. He noticed a
headline that mentioned the moon.

The moon, although he had never
been there, was Jerry's favorite
planet, because he had heard from
a reliable source that the moon was
made of green cheese. And cheese
—any color—was Jerry's favorite
food.

Jerry read the newspaper story
and got very excited. It said that
the first trip to the moon would be

Exciting Headlines

made by an animal. It also said that any animal who thought he was qualified should report to the Space Center. There an examination would be conducted, and one animal would be selected to make the first trip to the moon.

To Jerry, it was the opportunity of a lifetime! He could just see himself landing on the moon! He would be in his glory! What a feast he would have! The first day, he would stuff himself on green cheese plain. The next day, he would have

Opportunity of a Lifetime

it with cream and sugar. Then
green cheese soup! Then green
cheese pie and then green cheese
sandwiches! And finally, the finest
treat of all—a big, thick slice of
green cheese, between two big,
thick slices of green cheese, all
smothered in a green cheese sauce!

And, too, he told himself, he
would be doing a good thing for
science. Wouldn't all the world's
scientists be pleased when he returned from the trip to the moon
with proof that many good things

Finest Treat of All

to eat could be made out of green cheese?

There was no doubt in Jerry's mind that it was his duty to volunteer to go to the moon. With his tail twitching excitedly, he scampered from the house and headed for the Space Center!

Tom, who had been watching all this from a hiding place, cocked his head. He was completely baffled. What was Jerry up to? What kind of mischief was he getting into?

Off to the Space Center

Somehow, Tom decided, the newspaper had something to do with it. Still looking puzzled, he crept from his hiding place behind the big easy chair and approached the newspaper.

The minute Tom read the story about the selection of an animal to make the first trip to the moon, he knew exactly where Jerry had gone.

At first he was amused. Jerry didn't have a chance in the world to be chosen to go to the moon, he

Discovering Jerry's Plan

thought. But then, after consider-
ing for a moment, it didn't seem so
improbable. Jerry *was* an animal.
And, although he wasn't the smart-
est animal Tom had ever met, he
wasn't the *dumbest*, either. It *was*
possible that Jerry might be selected for the trip.

Good riddance, Tom decided. Let
him go to the moon! It sounded
dangerous. Jerry might not come
back. If he didn't, Tom would no
longer be bothered by Jerry's con-
stant troublemaking.

Good Riddance!

On the other hand, though, suppose Jerry did get to the moon and did get back? He would be a national hero! The President would present him with a medal! He would drive up Broadway in a limousine, with the crowds cheering and throwing ticker tape! And when he got back home . . . he would be King of the House!

Tom suddenly turned as green as a green cheese with envy and jealousy. Jerry a hero! King of the House! Tom could hardly stand it.

A Jealous Tom

Something had to be done. And
Tom, obviously, was the one who
had to do it!

The only way to keep Jerry from
becoming a hero, Tom decided, was
to see to it that he did not go to
the moon. Tom would have to make
sure that Jerry did not pass the
examination. That way, he could
never be selected.

Tom galloped from the house
and raced toward the Space Center. He was determined to stop
Jerry from becoming a hero!

Racing Toward the Space Center

Only Volunteers Are Allowed

CHAPTER 2

RELUCTANT VOLUNTEER

The Space Center was in a big building that was surrounded by a high wire fence. There was a guard at the gate. Tom told the guard he was there to visit a friend. But the guard replied that only animals who were volunteering to take the test could be allowed in.

Tom was desperate. If he was

going to keep Jerry from becoming
a hero, he had to get inside the
Space Center. So he signed up to
take the test, too. And the guard
opened the gate and let him in.

Inside the building, another
guard directed Tom to a huge room
where all the animals had gathered
to take the first test. Tom was surprised at the number of volunteers.
There were more animals in the
room than he had ever before seen
in one place.

He saw at least a dozen monkeys,

Ready for the Tests

a porcupine, a snake, a large number of squirrels, more guinea pigs than he could count, several dogs, and a great many other cats. And right smack-dab in the middle of the whole group was Jerry!

At that moment, the man who was to conduct the first test entered the room. He was a thin man with very large eyeglasses; he looked extremely intelligent. So Tom was not too surprised when the man told the animals to line up and then informed them that the

Volunteers

first test would be an intelligence test.

Tom made sure that he got into line right next to Jerry. Seeing Tom, Jerry looked a little leery. He wondered why Tom would want to go to the moon, because cheese did not happen to be Tom's favorite food.

"Attention, animals!" the examiner said. "I am going to pass out sets of numbers," he continued when the animals had become quiet. "The numbers will range from

"Attention."

one to ten, but they will be scrambled. I want you to sort them out. That is, I want you to put them in order, beginning with one and ending with ten. Is that clear?"

The animals indicated that they understood. Then the examiner began handing out the sets of numbers. When he finished, he blew a whistle and the sorting began.

Both Tom and Jerry got their numbers put in order very quickly. Soon, the examiner blew his whistle again. That was the signal that

The First Test

the time was up. Then he started walking down the line, checking to see if any of the animals had failed the test. He was disappointed to discover that one of the squirrels, instead of putting the numbers in order, had stuffed them into his cheeks, as if they were acorns.

Just before the examiner got to Jerry, Tom reached over and turned two of Jerry's numbers upside down.

Reaching Jerry, the examiner scowled. "That's not good," he said.

Changing Jerry's Number

"Don't you know the difference between a six and a nine? Your six is bottom-side-up, and your nine is topside-down."

Jerry looked flabbergasted. He was sure he had placed the six and the nine in the right places.

"No excuses!" the examiner said severely. Then he moved on to where Tom was standing. "Perfect!" he announced after he had inspected Tom's work.

Tom beamed.

Jerry looked angry. He could

"No Excuses!"

guess what had happened to his numbers.

"Now," the examiner said, addressing the animals again, "we will have a test that is a bit more difficult. I will distribute sets of letters. The letters, like the numbers, will be scrambled. Your task will be to make words of them."

The examiner gave each animal a set of letters, then blew his whistle once more. Quickly they began trying to form words.

Jerry got an *O*, an *M*, another *O*,

Scrambled Letters

and a *Z*. It took him only a second to make *ZOOM* out of the letters.

Tom found that he had an *O*, an *I*, another *O*, and an *H*. He studied the letters a minute, then made *IHOO* out of them. But that did not look much like any word he had ever seen before. So he tried again. This time, he made *HOOI*. That didn't look right, either, however. So, once again, he rearranged the letters. This time, he was satisfied. He had made *OHIO*.

Just then the whistle blew, and

Tom Completes the Test

the examiner began inspecting the animals' work.

Tom reached over and turned Jerry's *M* upside down so that it looked like a *W*.

This time, though, Jerry was expecting a trick. So he reached over and turned two of Tom's letters— the *H* and the *I*—upside down.

A second later the examiner reached Jerry. Unfortunately, Jerry had not had time to turn his *M* topside up.

"Too bad," the examiner said.

Changing Jerry's Word

"You misspelled that word. Everybody knows that *ZOW* is spelled with only one *O*. Yours is spelled *Z-O-O-W* instead of *Z-O-W*. You should have spelled *ZOOM* with your letters."

Jerry started to protest.

"No excuses!" the examiner said, moving on to where Tom was standing.

Well, Jerry thought, at least Tom's word would be wrong, too.

"Perfect again!" the examiner said, looking at Tom's word.

A Misspelling

Jerry could hardly believe what he heard. He knew that he had turned Tom's *H* and *I* upside down. Then he looked at Tom's word, and he understood. Even turned upside down, Tom's *H* and *I* were still topside up. *OHIO*, turned upside down, was still *OHIO*.

It Still Spells OHIO

Who Had the Best Score?

CHAPTER 3

TOM WINS AGAIN

When the intelligence test was finished, the brainy-looking examiner left, and all the animals began guessing which one had the best score.

They did not have much time to talk about it, for they soon heard a whistle blow again, and they saw that a new examiner had entered the room. The new man was dressed in a T-shirt, and his muscles bulged as if he were hiding grapefruit under his sleeves.

"Awright, youse guys," the examiner barked, "it's time to take the physical test. Follow me—I'm taking you to the gym!"

With the examiner leading the way, the animals trooped out of the room and down a long corridor. To the right and left they saw other rooms where space scientists were at work developing and testing

"Follow Me."

new space gadgets. Then they saw
a large dining hall. Next, they
passed a big kitchen.

It took Tom longer to get past
the kitchen than it did the other
animals, however. There he saw a
great mound of butter squares that
had been prepared to serve at
lunch, and he popped into the kitch-
en to pick up a few pats. He had
an idea that they might come in
handy when the animals got to the
gym. Somehow he had to make
absolutely sure that Jerry did not

A Few Pats of Butter

pass the physical test.

Finally the animals reached the gym. "The first test, youse guys," the examiner told them, "is to pull your own weight."

The animals lined up, and, one by one, they were weighed. Each one was then taken to a block of iron that weighed exactly as much as he did. Each block of iron had a chain attached to it. Each animal was told to pull the iron block a certain distance.

Some of the animals had trouble.

Jerry Weighs In

One of the squirrels couldn't even budge his block of iron. And one of the monkeys didn't even try. He thought the block of iron looked like the base of a statue, and he posed on his—looking like a statue of a monkey on a block of iron. He made all the animals laugh—but he also flunked the test.

Tom had no trouble at all pulling his block of iron. Then it was Jerry's turn. Jerry got a good grip on the chain and tugged, and the block began to move. It looked as

Pretending to Be a Statue

if he were going to pass the test
with no trouble at all.

However, Tom saw a chance to
use one of the pats of butter he had
brought from the kitchen. Pretending to be cheering Jerry on, he
came up to him and dropped one
of the pats of butter in his path.

All of a sudden Jerry began slipping and sliding. His hind feet flew
out from under him, and—*splat*—
he was suddenly sitting down!
Jerry scrambled determinedly to
his feet. Once more he tugged at

Slipping and Sliding

the weight. And again his feet went flying in several different directions, and—*whomp*—he found himself sitting when he should have been standing.

"Time's up!" the examiner announced. "Sorry, buster," he said to Jerry. "Maybe you didn't hear me right. This was a pulling test, not a sitting test!"

Tom thought that was the funniest joke he had heard in a long time. He doubled over with hearty laughter.

"Time's Up!"

"Next comes the rope climb," the examiner told the animals, leading them to a spot where a long rope was dangling down from a beam of the ceiling. "I'll blow my whistle, and you'll start to climb. If you make it to the top before I blow my whistle again, you'll pass the test."

Jerry quickly volunteered to go first. That way, he hoped, Tom would not have time to play a trick on him. And he was right. When the examiner tooted the whistle,

Ready for the Rope Climb

Jerry got a good grip on the rope with all four paws and went zipping up to the top, paw over paw over paw over paw, and reached it before the whistle blew the second time.

"That's the way to do it!" the examiner said. "Okay—next!"

One by one the animals began clambering up the rope. It was easy for most of them. The dogs and the guinea pigs couldn't even get a start, though, and so they failed the test.

Jerry Zips to the Top

While the others were taking the rope-climbing test, Jerry went back to the spot where he had failed the weight-pulling test. Then he discovered why he had failed. He found butter on the floor.

Jerry had a pretty good idea how the butter had gotten there, and when he returned to where the other animals were gathered, he saw the pats of butter in Tom's paw. Jerry knew he was right.

That made him eager to get even with Tom. He waited until it was

Why He Failed

Tom's turn to climb the rope. Then, pretending to be wishing him luck, he went up to Tom and shook his paw. When they shook, of course, the butter was smeared all over Tom's paw.

The examiner tooted the whistle. Tom got a grip on the rope and began to climb. But his paws slipped.

"Get going!" the examiner barked.

Paw over paw, Tom tried to climb the rope. He got partway

Slippery Paws

up—and then began slipping. Down he slid!

Unfortunately, the next animal in line was waiting at the bottom of the rope. That animal happened to be the porcupine.

Slipping, Tom landed on the porcupine's sharp quills. He let out a shriek! Then, spurred on by the quills, up the rope he scrambled!

"Wow!" the examiner cried. "A world's record!"

Jerry groaned. Tom had won again!

A Painful Landing

Mysterious Steel Boxes

CHAPTER 4

THE ISOLATION TEST

After the physical test, the animals were taken to a different room. When they reached it, they looked puzzled and began asking each other questions, but, of course, they didn't have any answers.

What baffled the animals was the great number of big steel boxes in the room. All the boxes looked alike—a lot like very serious play-houses. Each one had a door, but none had a window. There was a pipe connected to each box at the rear.

A few minutes later, a quite thin and very nervous-looking man entered the room.

"I'm in charge of the isolation test," he said, trembling. "We want to find out if you can stand being alone for a long period of time, because the trip to the moon will be a long and lonely trip."

"I'm in Charge."

The animals were beginning to understand what the boxes were for.

"Each animal will enter one of these compartments," the examiner said, pointing to the boxes. "You will stay inside for a whole day. Inside, you will find food capsules, so you won't get hungry. Once you enter the compartment, you will begin hearing sounds. These are the sounds you will probably hear on the trip to the moon. They will be soft, soothing sounds.

"Each Animal Will Enter One."

After a while, you'll get so tired of hearing them, you'll probably want to scream."

The animals giggled.

"Stop that!" the examiner screamed. "I can't stand soft, soothing sounds!"

The animals became quiet.

"The ones who stay in the compartments for twenty-four hours will pass the test," the examiner continued. "The ones who don't, won't. There's no need to fret about how the loneliness will affect you,

"Stop That!"

though. I've spent many a day in
those compartments, and I'm as
normal as anybody—when I'm ly-
ing down and have a cold cloth
on my head."

Each of the animals entered a
compartment, then the examiner
closed all the doors. After that, he
left to get a cold cloth for his head
and to lie down.

As soon as the examiner had
gone, Tom slipped out of his compartment. He thought that if he
could scare Jerry, he could chase

Time to Begin the Test

him out into the open, and Jerry
would fail the test.

Tom began banging on the side
of Jerry's compartment. He hit it
and he kicked it and he pounded on
it—but Jerry did not come out.

Next, Tom loosened the pipe that
was connected to Jerry's compartment. Then he began making ghost
sounds.

"Whoooooooooeeeeee!" he howled.

He expected Jerry to come racing out, thinking that his compartment was haunted, but, to Tom's

Jerry Doesn't Come Out

surprise, Jerry did not appear.

Tom tried to think of a different way to frighten Jerry. Nothing came to mind immediately, however. So he returned to his own compartment to give the matter some further thought.

Meanwhile, Jerry was having a great time inside his compartment laughing to himself. He knew, of course, that it was Tom who had been pounding on the side of his compartment and making the ghost sounds. He was a bit disappointed,

Enjoying Himself

in fact, when the noise stopped. It had kept him from getting lonely.

After a while, Jerry decided to do the same thing to Tom that Tom had tried to do to him—to chase him out of his compartment and make him fail the test.

Jerry opened the door of his box and looked out. Tom was nowhere in sight. Looking around, Jerry spotted a fire hose hanging on the wall. It was just the thing to use, he decided, to flush Tom out of his compartment.

Spotting the Fire Hose

Jerry attached the hose to the hydrant. Then he removed the pipe that was connected to Tom's compartment. Next, he poked the nozzle of the hose in through the hole where the pipe had been, and then turned on the water full force.

Enjoying himself, Jerry waited for Tom to come rushing out. He waited and he waited, but Tom's door did not open. Jerry began to get a little worried. Suppose Tom, for some reason, *couldn't* get out!

Surprise for Tom

In a sudden panic, Jerry rushed
to the door of Tom's compartment
and yanked it open. Instead of
Tom, a great rush of water came
out!

The wall of water swept Jerry out
of the room, out of the building, and
through the Space Center entrance.
The water poured into a stream,
taking Jerry with it. Frantic, Jerry
grabbed out, trying to catch hold
of something. But all he got was a
pawful of water. Finally the stream
flowed into a river. Luckily for

A Wall of Water

Jerry there were a lot of logs in the river, and he was able to scramble aboard one and then scamper to shore.

He found, however, that he was a long way from the Space Center. It would take, he realized gloomily, almost twenty-four hours to get back.

After a long, weary trudge, Jerry reached the room where the isolation test was being given. The examiner was there and the test had just ended.

Scrambling Aboard a Log

"Couldn't stand the loneliness, eh?" the examiner said to Jerry. "Had to go out for a walk in the fresh air, I see. Too bad. You can't do that, you know, in space."

Just then, Tom emerged from his compartment. He looked a little water-logged. But he had passed the test.

"You Can't Do That in Space."

The New Examiner

CHAPTER 5

ASTRONAUT ACROBATICS

As soon as the isolation test was over, the very nervous examiner left to go lie down and put a cold cloth on his head.

A few minutes later, a different examiner entered the room. He was so skinny, he looked as if he couldn't weigh more than a pound and a half, clothes and all.

"I'm here to give you the weightlessness test," the new examiner said. "If you'll just follow me, we'll go to the testing ground."

The examiner led the way and the whole group trooped out of the building. They soon arrived at a small open area. Floating above the area was a fairly large balloon. A long, stout cord was attached to the balloon to keep it from floating away.

"When you get to the moon," the examiner told the animals, "your

Painting a Crooked Line

stopped, and Jerry stepped off.

"Now, draw the line," the examiner commanded.

Jerry took in a deep breath to steady himself. He felt a little dizzy—but not too much. He picked up the paint can and the brush and started painting a line.

He was painting a fairly straight line—much better than the monkey had done. But all of a sudden he was startled by a flash of light— and he zigged. His line was no longer as straight as it had been.

A Flash of Light

Very carefully, Jerry continued. But once more a light flashed in his eyes. This time he zagged.

Looking up, Jerry saw what was happening. Tom had a mirror and was using it to flash a light in Jerry's eyes!

Grimly Jerry carried on, painting the line and trying to duck the flashes of light at the same time. But when he finished, his line looked as if it had been painted by the crooked man who walked the crooked mile.

"I'll Let the Balloon Go."

shot up into the sky, with Jerry, strapped into the harness, hanging down below.

Then, all of a sudden, the balloon reached the end of the cord and jerked to a stop. Jerry bobbed about in space like a mouse on a string.

"Do what I tell you, now," the examiner called to Jerry. "First, let's see if you can touch your ears with your toes."

Jerry was tempted to tell the examiner that he wasn't interested

Waiting for Instructions

in going to the moon to touch his ears with his toes—that he was only interested in the green cheese. But he didn't want to fail the test. So he did what the examiner told him to do.

"Very good," the examiner said. "Now, let's see you do a forward somersault."

Tom, who was watching all this, was not very happy. It looked as though Jerry would be able to pass the test very easily.

So, just as Jerry started to do

Touching His Ear With His Toe

the forward somersault, Tom gave the cord that was attached to the balloon a sudden tug.

Instead of performing a forward somersault, Jerry did a combination backward somersault, handstand and swan dive.

"No! No! No!" the examiner cried. "That's all wrong!"

The examiner kept telling Jerry what to do, and Jerry kept trying. But Tom yanked on the cord every time, and Jerry ended up doing everything but the right thing.

Tom Yanks the Cord

Finally, shaking his head in disgust, the examiner pulled the balloon down and released Jerry from the harness.

Tom was next to take the test. The examiner strapped him in, then sent Tom and the balloon aloft.

"Touch the tip of your left ear with the tip of your tail!" the examiner called up to Tom.

Tom did it perfectly.

"Now," the examiner called to Tom, "I want you to do these

Tom Goes Aloft

things, one after the other: pretend to climb a wall, fly like a bird, dive into a pool, walk a tightwire, slide down a hill on your nose, and ride a bicycle no-hands."

Meanwhile, Jerry had been wondering how to get even with Tom for spoiling his chance to pass the test. At that very moment an idea occurred to him. As Tom began doing the things the examiner ordered, Jerry got the cord that was fastened to the balloon in his teeth and bit right through it.

Getting Even

The balloon, of course, began rising, floating higher and higher.

"Runaway balloon!" the examiner cried.

Tom saw what was happening, and he was scared out of his wits. Frantic, he began climbing the harness. He reached the balloon. His claws sank into it. There was a loud pop! The balloon had burst! Tom was falling straight down!

Terrified, Tom began grabbing out, trying to catch hold of something, anything, in order to halt

The Balloon Bursts

the fall and avoid a hard landing.

With all that twisting and turning and grasping, Tom looked exactly like he was climbing a wall,
flying like a bird, diving into a
pool, walking a tightrope, sliding
downhill on his nose, and riding a
bicycle no-hands, all at the same
time.

"Marvelous!" the watching examiner exclaimed.

Tom crashed to earth!

The examiner and the other animals rushed up to him and helped

A Long Fall

him to his feet. He was a little groggy, but unhurt.

"Congratulations!" the examiner told Tom. "You passed the test with climbing, riding, diving, walking, sliding, and flying colors!"

"Congratulations!"

The Animals Are Puzzled

CHAPTER 6

WHIRLIGIG WOES

As soon as all the animals had taken the weightlessness test, the examiner led them back into the building and left them in another room.

They were puzzled by what they found in the room. There was an apparatus that looked a lot like a big, upside-down dinner plate.

When they looked at it more closely, they discovered that it could be turned by an attached motor.

What baffled them even more, though, was the full can of paint and the paintbrush that were sitting beside the machine. The animals couldn't figure out what these things had to do with the platelike machine.

Their questions were soon answered. Another examiner entered the room. He was average-looking, but he did seem to have some

Part of the Test?

peculiarities. He stumbled around a bit. And his eyes looked somewhat glazed.

"This is the dizziness test," the examiner announced. "The spacecraft you will ride to the moon may do a lot of tumbling and turning in space. So, if possible, we want to find an animal who will not get dizzy too easily."

The animals all began telling each other that they *never* got dizzy, even if they turned around and around a hundred times.

"This Is the Dizziness Test."

"Quiet!" the examiner ordered.

Then he explained the apparatus that looked like an upside-down dinner plate.

"This machine turns," he said. "It can be made to turn slow or fast. The faster it goes, the dizzier you will get. You will mount it, each one at a time, and then be spun around."

That sounded like fun.

"As soon as the machine stops," the examiner continued, "you will get off. Then you will take this

"You Will Be Spun Around."

bucket of paint and this paintbrush, and you will attempt to
paint a straight line. If you can do
it, you will pass the test. But if you
paint a crooked line, you will fail.
All clear?"

The animals replied that they
understood. Most of them said that
the test sounded easy.

One of the monkeys was the first
to get on the machine. It started
spinning slowly, then it speeded up.
The other animals laughed, watching the monkey trying to hold on.

First to Try

Suddenly the machine stopped. The monkey climbed off, picked up the paint and the brush, and began painting a line. But he was so dizzy that he stumbled all over, and the line he painted wiggled and waggled this way and that.

Jerry was the second one to take the test. He got aboard the machine, and it began whirling him around. He had to lie as flat as he could to keep from sliding off. Just as he felt himself beginning to slip, the machine slowed down. Then it

"Now the Weightlessness Test."

weight won't be of much use to
you. It won't hold you down as well
as it does here on earth. On the
moon, for instance, if you make a
high jump, it may be hours before
you come down again."

To the animals, that sounded
like a great deal of fun.

"So," the examiner went on, "the
purpose of this test is to find out
how well you can handle yourselves
while you're floating free."

The examiner chose Jerry to be
the first one to take the test. He

Explaining the Test

got hold of the cord and pulled the balloon down to earth. The animals then saw that the balloon had a kind of harness attached to it.

"I'm going to strap you into this harness," the examiner said to Jerry, strapping him into the harness. "Then I'm going to let the balloon go, and you'll be dangling down below it."

Jerry was about to ask what he was supposed to do then, but, at that moment, the examiner released the cord on the balloon. It

Tom Uses a Mirror

"Too bad," the examiner said, shaking his head. "And you had such a fine start, too."

When it was Tom's turn to get aboard the whirligig, Jerry had already figured out how to get back at him.

The machine started, and Tom began turning. He was grinning broadly, because the test was so easy for him that he didn't even have to hold on.

However, Tom had a surprise coming to him. As the whirligig

An Easy Test

began to revolve faster, Jerry
sneaked over to the lever that controlled the speed and pushed it as
far as it would go.

Suddenly the whirligig was spinning as fast as it could turn. Tom
was whirling around at such a rate
of speed that he looked more like
a blur than a cat.

"Yowwwrrrl!" Tom yelped. He
tried desperately to hold on.

"Runaway whirligig!" the examiner cried, running toward the control to stop the machine. But he

Full Speed

stumbled over his own feet and fell flat on his face.

Tom was sliding toward the edge of the spinning whirligig. Frantically he tried to crawl back toward the center.

The examiner scrambled to his feet, stumbled again, and went diving at the lever that controlled the speed.

But he reached it a second too late. Tom suddenly went flying from the machine, and he shot through the air like a rocket. In

Shooting Through the Air

panic, he grabbed out—and got hold of the paintbrush. The line of paint he left behind was as straight as a yardstick!

Tom and the paintbrush collided with a wall and came to an abrupt halt.

The examiner, amazed by the absolute straightness of Tom's line, rushed over to him and raised his paw in the air.

"The champ!" the examiner cried.

"The Champ!"

Another Examiner Enters

CHAPTER 7

OUTSMARTED

As soon as the animals had completed the dizziness test, they were directed to a new examiner.

He was the sort of man who was so ordinary-looking that he could have been mistaken for at least a half-dozen other people—except for one thing. His eyes were different. They looked like two little bright, shiny buttons; one was red and the other was green. And, in the right light, one seemed to say GO and one seemed to say STOP.

"I'm in charge of showing you how to use the computers aboard our spacecraft," the man informed the animals. "Computers, as you probably know, are machines that do much of our work and thinking for us. Our computers are operated by punching buttons."

The examiner then led the animals to a large room in which there

"I'm in Charge of Computers."

was a huge machine. It had a happy face painted on it to make it look human. Nevertheless, there was no mistaking the fact that it was a machine, for although it had a face, it had no ears.

At the front of the machine, there was a big control board. On the board there were hundreds of sets of buttons in many different colors. There were red buttons, blue buttons, orange buttons, black buttons, pink buttons, and white buttons.

Explaining the Control Board

"When you're aboard the space-craft, heading for the moon, it will be necessary for you to operate some of the controls," the examiner told the animals. "The purpose of this test is to find out how well you can follow commands."

The examiner then told one of the monkeys to go to the control board.

"I'll tell you what buttons to punch," he said. "If you do it right, nothing will happen. But if you do it wrong—look out!"

Following Commands

Then the examiner began barking commands. "Red buttons!" he snapped.

The monkey aimed a finger at the red buttons. But at that same moment the examiner snapped another command, "Blue buttons!"

The monkey got so confused that instead of punching the red buttons or the blue buttons, he punched the white buttons. Instantly the machine shot him right square between the eyes with a squirt of water!

The Wrong Button

"That's what happens," the examiner said happily.

He then told the animals how important it was to punch the right buttons. "The spacecraft might go off course," he said, "if, in flight, the wrong button is pushed."

Tom, however, was not listening very closely. Since Jerry was next in line to be tested, Tom was busy making sure that he would fail. He found that the colored tops could be removed from the buttons. So he changed them around, putting

Switching the Button Tops

red tops on blue buttons, and blue tops on red buttons, and so on.

"Next!" the examiner said.

Jerry stepped up to the machine, and the examiner began issuing commands. "Red buttons!" he snapped.

Jerry punched red. But, of course, what he actually got was blue—and a squirt of water.

"Try again," the examiner said. "Black buttons!"

Jerry quickly punched black. Because of Tom's trickery, however,

A Squirt of Water

what he *really* got was white—and another squirt.

"That's the worst job of button-punching I've ever seen," the examiner declared.

Then he again told the animals how important it was to punch the right buttons.

While the examiner was speaking, Tom hurriedly put all the button tops back where they belonged. This time, though, Jerry saw him. And he realized why the wrong thing had happened when the right

Replacing the Button Tops

buttons had been punched.

Jerry thought for a second and came up with a plan. Making sure that Tom saw what he was doing, he pretended to change the button tops the same way that Tom had. In fact, though, he didn't change them at all.

"Your turn," the examiner said, pointing to Tom.

Tom stepped up to the machine.

"Red buttons!" the examiner ordered.

Tom had no trouble spotting the

Jerry Tries a Plan

set of red buttons. He thought, however, that Jerry had switched the tops and that the red buttons were really the blue buttons.

That wasn't all that was going through his mind, though. He was beginning to worry. So far, he had passed all the tests. And that was *not* why he had come to the Space Center. All he had wanted was to make Jerry fail. So he decided to stop being so good at taking tests.

When Tom heard the examiner

A Confident Tom

command him to punch the red buttons, that was exactly what he did. He thought that Jerry had changed the tops and that, as a result, he would really be punching the blue buttons.

Tom waited for the squirt of water. But nothing happened, because the button beneath the red top was really a red button.

"Perfect!" the examiner said. "Let's try it again. Blue buttons!"

Quickly Tom punched a blue button, thinking it was really a red

Nothing Happens

button hidden under a blue top.

There was no squirt of water.

"You did it again!" the examiner beamed, congratulating Tom.

Tom drooped. He certainly had done it again. Somehow he had outsmarted himself. But how?

"You Did It Again."

Who Will Make the Moon Trip?

CHAPTER 8

THE COLLECTORS

When the button-punching test was completed, the animals were told to remain in the room with the large machine.

While they waited they discussed which animal had the best chance of being chosen to take the trip to the moon.

Each of the monkeys thought he

would be picked, even though none of them had passed any of the tests. They reasoned, however, that anybody who would take the first trip to the moon had to be a little crazy. And who was crazier than a monkey?

A few moments later another examiner entered the room. He looked a little like the first examiner they had seen. He also wore large eyeglasses and looked very brainy. They knew he was a different man, because he was carrying

Paper Bags for the Next Test

an armload of paper bags, and the first examiner hadn't carried any.

The examiner distributed the paper bags, giving one to each animal; then he told them about the next test.

"The idea," he said, "is to find out what kind of scientific judgment you have. The animal who goes to the moon will be expected to bring back a lot of specimens for the earth scientists to study."

One of the monkeys asked if specimens meant coconuts.

"A Scientific Judgment Test."

Jerry laughed to himself. The monkey apparently thought that the moon was made of coconuts instead of green cheese.

"I won't answer that," the examiner replied. "The purpose of this test is to discover if you know a right specimen from a wrong specimen."

The examiner then told the animals to leave the building and go out onto the grounds. They would have an hour to collect specimens, he said. At the end of the time, he

Off to Collect Specimens

would blow a whistle. Then he would examine their specimens and decide which animal had the best scientific judgment.

The animals rushed from the building, carrying their bags. All except Tom, that is. He had no intention of passing any more tests. He knew that the best way to fail this test was not to collect any specimens at all. So, when the others left, Tom curled up for a one-hour catnap.

Outside on the grounds, Jerry

Ready for a Catnap

was scampering from here to there and from there to here, examining everything he found and deciding whether or not it was a good specimen to collect.

He knew, of course, that he wouldn't find any green cheese. He would have to wait until he got to the moon for that. He guessed, though, that what the examiner considered a good specimen would surely be anything that in any way looked like green cheese. In other words—anything green.

Collecting Anything Green

The first thing that Jerry put into his bag was a twig that still had some green leaves attached to it.

Next, he came across a stone that was covered with green moss. Into the bag it went.

A few minutes later, he spotted a green grasshopper. He began chasing it all over the grounds— hopping along behind it—trying to get it to hop into the bag. Finally, just as the whistle blew, he captured it.

A Lively Specimen

All the animals hurried back into the building. The noise they made awakened Tom. He yawned and stretched and then got i. to line right beside Jerry.

The line had just formed when the examiner entered the room.

"Bags open!" he commanded. "Let's see what you've collected."

Then he began going from animal to animal, looking into each bag as he moved down the line.

One of the monkeys was first in line. In his bag, the examiner

"Bags Open!"

found a shiny doorknob, a foot-scraper, and an empty soda bottle.

"Not what I had in mind," the examiner said sourly.

While Jerry was watching and listening, interested in what the other animals had collected, Tom was peeking into his bag. He saw the twig with the leaves, the moss-covered rock, and the grasshopper.

Tom did not know whether the examiner would approve of these specimens or not, but he was not going to take any chances. Very

Checking Jerry's Bag

sneakily he began tearing an opening in the bottom of Jerry's bag.

Just before the examiner reached Jerry, Tom finished tearing the hole. Jerry's specimens dropped to the floor!

The examiner leaned over and peered into Jerry's bag. "Nothing!" he said, surprised.

Baffled, Jerry looked into the bag. It was completely empty!

" 'Nothing' is not quite good enough," the examiner said gruffly. "Why bother to send *you* to the

Empty!

moon at all if you came back with absolutely nothing?"

The examiner moved on to Tom. "Marvelous!" he exclaimed.

It was Tom's turn to be surprised —until he looked down and saw what the examiner had seen.

When Tom had torn the hole in Jerry's bag, the specimens had dropped near Tom's feet. The examiner assumed that Tom had collected the twig with the leaves, the moss-covered rock, and the grasshopper.

"Marvelous!"

"A plant, a mineral, and an insect—*exactly* what we'd like to have from the moon," the examiner said. "That's the best collection yet!"

Tom wished he had never awakened from his nap.

"The Best Collection Yet!"

A Jolly Examiner

CHAPTER 9

NO-FUN FUN HOUSE

The examiner who was in charge of the next test was a big, round, smiling, jolly-looking fellow. Just by looking at him, the animals guessed that the next test was going to be fun.

Chuckling, the examiner motioned for the animals to follow him, and he led them out of the main building and across the grounds to a smaller building.

When the animals saw the sign over the entrance to the smaller building, they were positive that the new test would be fun, for the sign said FUN HOUSE.

"Animals," the grinning examiner said, "of all the tests you've taken, this final test is the most important. So listen closely to what I tell you."

The animals all leaned forward, eager to hear every word. But Tom

A Fun Test

was not listening. Since he wasn't interested in passing the test, he didn't care whether or not he heard.

"What exactly do we know about what we'll find on the moon?" the chuckling examiner asked. "Why, for all we know," he went on, grinning, "we'll find the moon inhabited by monsters."

The animals suddenly looked a little worried.

"And not just ordinary, everyday monsters, either," the examiner said cheerfully. "They may be

"We May Find Moon Monsters."

hideous, man-eating, cat-eating, monkey-eating, or mouse-eating monsters!"

All the animals, except Tom, shuddered. What did Tom care? *He* wasn't going to the moon.

"So," the examiner continued, grinning from ear to ear, "this final test will introduce you to some of the monsters you may meet on the moon. It will also give us a chance to find out how you would handle such monsters."

One of the monkeys asked the

Tom Isn't Worried

examiner if he meant that there were hideous, man-eating, monkey-eating, mouse-eating monsters inside the Fun House.

Doubling over with laughter, the examiner replied, "Yessiree! There sure are!"

When they heard that, three of the monkeys, two of the cats, and all the mice except Jerry suddenly remembered they had left something cooking on their stoves at home. They rushed off to take care of their cooking.

A Frightened Group

The examiner laughed so hard at the departing animals, that it was a full five minutes before he could say anything.

When he finally got control of himself, he said, "Well, who'll be first to meet the monsters?"

One of the squirrels raised a paw to ask a question, but the examiner thought he was volunteering to be first. So the giggling man shoved the squirrel through the Fun House doorway.

"Now comes the fun part!" the

The First Volunteer

examiner told the other animals.

About a minute later, the squirrel came rushing out. He was so scared that his fur had turned white. He was so frightened, in fact, that he didn't even stop to find out if he had passed the test! He went racing across the grounds. It looked as if he would never stop running.

The examiner howled with laughter. "That's why we call it the Fun House," he told the other animals. "Isn't this fun?"

Racing Out the Door

Jerry was picked to enter the Fun House next. Trembling, he stepped inside. It was pitch black. But a moment later a light flashed on, and all of a sudden a huge, horned, bug-eyed, green-skinned monster reared up in front of him!

Jerry was so frightened that he very nearly turned tail and ran. Just then the monster disappeared.

Step by step, shaking, Jerry moved on. A second later, the light flashed again, and another monster popped up in front of him. This one

A Frightening Sight

was purple and it had the body of an alligator, the head of a lion, the arms of an octopus, and the claws of a vulture.

As frightened as he was, though, Jerry noticed something else about the monster. It had sprung a spring, and the spring was protruding from its ear. Jerry realized at once that the monster was only a mechanical monster and that it couldn't possibly hurt him.

From then on, although hideous-looking monsters popped out from

A Mechanical Monster

everywhere, Jerry walked through the Fun House without any fear at all.

When Jerry emerged, the examiner looked very unhappy. Somehow, the Fun House wasn't much fun any more—for him, anyway.

The examiner chose Tom to enter the Fun House next.

Shortly after Tom went inside, the examiner and the other animals heard a terrified scream. It was obvious that Tom had met a monster. The first scream was soon

An Unhappy Examiner

followed by a horrifying shriek.
Then there were a crash, a clatter,
and a bang. All of a sudden one of
the walls of the Fun House col-
lapsed! Then the front fell down!
The examiner and the animals saw
Tom and the monsters inside. Tom
was dashing about frantically,
crashing into one monster after
another and leaving mechanical
parts in his path—heads here,
claws there, jaws here, tails there.
Tom had destroyed them all!

The examiner broke into tears.

Tom Is Frantic

The Fun House was a ruin and a shambles.

"You failed the test!" the examiner cried, addressing Tom. "You spoiled all the fun!"

"You Failed the Test!"

Ready to Choose the Winner

CHAPTER 10

LAST LAUGH

Since the Fun House was the final test, the animals who remained were taken to an office in the main building.

The examiner at the Fun House told them that he and the other examiners were going to have a conference to decide which animal would have the honor of making the first trip to the moon. He asked them to wait in the office, telling them that he would return soon to give them the decision.

As soon as the examiner left, the animals all gathered together and tried to decide which one of them would be picked.

One of the monkeys said that he didn't think it would matter that he had failed all the tests. He still thought he would be picked because he was crazier than any of the other animals.

Confident He Will Win

But the porcupine told him that he was crazy if he thought he would be chosen because he was crazy.

After a lot of talk, the animals finally decided that either Tom or Jerry would be selected to take the trip to the moon. Tom had done best in most of the tests. On the other hand, Jerry was the only one who hadn't been scared by the monsters, and the examiner had said that the Fun House test was the most important of all the tests.

"Tom or Jerry Will Be Chosen."

"Well," the monkey said, "if it's going to be either that cat or that mouse, why should I wait around here for nothing? I'm not *that* crazy."

The monkey left. After thinking things over again, the other animals decided that he was right. They departed, too.

Only Tom and Jerry remained. But Tom was there only bodily. He had become so bored by all the talk about who had and who hadn't passed the tests, that he had

The Animals Depart

dropped off to sleep. He was sure, anyway, that he wouldn't be picked, because he had failed the final test so badly when he had made a shambles of the Fun House. Tom was just waiting around to have a good laugh when Jerry found out that he had failed, too, and wouldn't be going to the moon.

While Tom snoozed, Jerry began pacing about the office. Mounted on the walls were a number of big, closeup photographs of the moon that had been taken by a

Studying a Moon Photo

camera attached to a telescope.

Jerry began studying the photographs so that he would know exactly what green cheese looked like when—and if—he got to the moon.

But the closer he looked, the more puzzled he became. To him, the moon looked like rock with a covering of dust. It certainly didn't look like anything that could be made into a green cheese sandwich or a big bowl of green cheese soup.

Then, at the bottom of one of the

It Looks Like Rock and Dust

photographs, Jerry found some printing. When he read it, he discovered that his eyes had been right—*the moon was not made of green cheese!*

As far as Jerry was concerned, that was that! He had no more desire to be the first animal to take a trip to the moon. Tiptoeing, he headed toward the door.

At that very moment, however, the door flew open and the examiner who had been in charge of the Fun House test entered.

The Examiner Returns

"Where did everybody go?" the examiner asked.

The sound of his voice awakened Tom. He sat up.

"Well, no matter," the examiner said, chuckling, "because I see that our winner is still here."

Both Tom and Jerry looked disappointed. They both guessed that Jerry had won. Jerry was no longer interested in going to the moon, and Tom thought that all his efforts to make Jerry fail the tests had been for nothing.

Tom Is Awakened

"It was very close," the examiner told them. "Tom, up until the very last test, you had the top score. As I told you, though, that final test was the most important."

Tom looked even sadder than before. He was positive now that Jerry would get to the moon and would become a hero. He gritted his teeth, trying not to show his jealousy.

At the same time, Jerry was turning a little green, too, but not because of jealousy. He was having

A Jealous Tom

second thoughts. Since the moon was not made of green cheese, he was beginning to worry about the danger involved in making a space flight.

"It was a difficult decision for us to make," the examiner said. "We thought about it and thought about it, and talked and argued, and then all of a sudden we realized that we'd made a mistake."

Tom and Jerry looked at him with puzzled expressions on their faces.

"It Was a Difficult Decision."

"We'd been thinking that Jerry had done best on the Fun House test," the examiner explained. "After all, he was the only one who wasn't the least bit frightened by the monsters."

Tom and Jerry looked at each other and wondered what was coming next.

"But we were wrong," the examiner continued. "When Tom came face to face with those monsters, he tore into them and ripped them limb from limb. That's the kind of

Wondering What Is Next

animal we need on the moon—an animal who can handle those monsters and make the moon safe for people!"

Tom looked a little sick.

"You're the winner!" the examiner told him. "You leave for the moon in the morning!"

Tom made a dash for the door, but the examiner caught him and dragged him off.

"It'll be fun! Fun! Fun! *Fun!*" the examiner told Tom.

It was Jerry who was having all

A Reluctant Winner

the fun, though. He was rolling on the floor—having the last laugh—while Tom was hauled off for his trip to the moon!

The Last Laugh

Other **BIG LITTLE BOOKS**® Available

WHITMAN® *Classics*

Books for Your Permanent Library

BLACK BEAUTY

LITTLE WOMEN

HEIDI

HEIDI GROWS UP

TOM SAWYER

HUCKLEBERRY FINN

THE CALL OF THE WILD

TREASURE ISLAND

ALICE IN WONDERLAND

THE WONDERFUL WIZARD OF OZ

FAMOUS FAIRY TALES

ALGONQUIN

TALES OF POE

WHITMAN® *Full-Length Adventures*

Sports Stories

CELLAR TEAM (baseball)

BASKET FEVER (basketball)

PLAYERS' CHOICE (football)

DRAG STRIP DANGER (racing)

Short Story Collections

ADVENTURE CALLING (outdoor stories)

SHUDDERS (ghost stories)

GOLDEN PRIZE (horse stories)

THAT'S OUR CLEO! (cat stories)

WAY OUT (science fiction stories)

LIKE IT IS (stories for girls)

A BATCH OF THE BEST
(stories for girls)
